Graphic design and illustrations: Zapp
Story adaptation: Robyn Bryant

© 1994 Tormont Publications Inc.
   338 Saint Antoine St. East
   Montreal, Canada   H2Y 1A3
   Tel. (514) 954-1441
   Fax (514) 954-5086

ISBN 2-89429-505-7

Printed in China

THE BRAVE LITTLE TAILOR

TORMONT

Once upon a time, a little tailor was sitting at his workbench, sewing, when he heard a woman's voice in the street below.

"Jam for sale," the woman called.

Sticking his head out the window, the tailor shouted, "Up here, my good woman. I'll buy your jam."

The woman carried her heavy basket all
the way up three flights of stairs to the tailor's
room, and laid out all the jams and jellies.

The tailor opened every single lid and sniffed
each kind. Finally he said, "I'll buy three
spoonfuls of this one."

The woman was disappointed to sell such a small amount, but she measured it out and went on her way.

The tailor spread the jam on some bread, and put it down beside him. "I'll eat it as soon as I finish this shirt," he said to himself.

The smell of the jam soon attracted a number of flies. "Get out of here!" the tailor yelled. But the flies didn't understand his language and kept buzzing round the jam.

Finally the angry tailor struck at them with a piece of cloth. Seven flies fell to the ground, dead.

"Seven. That's amazing!" the little tailor said. "The whole world should know about this!"

So he made himself a leather belt, and on it he wrote SEVEN WITH ONE BLOW.

Then he put on his new belt and headed out into the world.

On the way out, he grabbed an old piece of cheese, and stuck it in his pocket in case he got hungry later.

Just outside the door, he found a bird, and for no special reason he stuck that in his pocket, too.

Outside of town, he came across a terrible looking giant. "Hello there," said the tailor. "I am going to seek my fortune in the wide world. Would you care to join me?"

The giant just laughed. "Don't be silly, you little crumb!"

The tailor was annoyed. "Look at my belt if you want to see what kind of man I am!" he said.

When the giant read the words on the belt, he thought the tailor had killed seven men. Still, he couldn't quite believe such a small man could be so strong, so he decided to test him.

The giant picked up a rock and squeezed it until water ran out. "I bet you can't do that," he said.

The tailor took the old cheese out of his pocket and squeezed it until whey came out.

The giant was not convinced. So he threw the rock far into the distance. "Try that," he said.

"Not bad," the tailor said. "But I notice it fell back down to earth." Then he pulled the bird from his pocket and threw it in the air. The bird, pleased to be free, flew out of sight.

"Well, if you're so strong,
help me carry this tree," the giant said,
pointing to a huge oak.

"Certainly," said the tailor. "You take
the trunk, and I'll carry the fat end,
which is no doubt much heavier."

The giant, walking in front, could not
see the tailor riding in the branches.

After a while, the giant said, "I'm tired. I have to put it down for a minute."

The tailor quickly jumped down and grabbed the branches to make it look as if he had been carrying the tree all along. "I guess you're not as strong as you thought," he said.

They walked on until they came to a cherry tree covered with fruit. The best cherries were at the top, so the giant bent the tree over for the tailor to pick some.

But when the little tailor grabbed hold of the top branch, the tree straightened up, flinging him right over the top.

"You can't even hold down a little branch?" said the giant.

"Of course I can," the tailor said. "I jumped over the tree on purpose. See if you can."

The giant tried to jump over, but got his foot caught in the branches.

Just then the king and his attendants came riding by. "What's this?" the king asked.

"Why nothing much, Sir. I've just captured this giant," said the tailor.

Since the giant had been a great nuisance in the neighborhood, the king rewarded the tailor with a bag of gold.

Soon, everyone in the land had heard about the brave little tailor who captured the giant.

And so the little tailor found fame and fortune and lived happily ever after.

29